For my two treasured wisecrackers,
Penny and Grace! — B.W.

For David, who stole my heart...and the last
piece of chocolate on my desk — M.T.

crackerjack
Jack

Written by **Bowman Wilker**
Illustrations by **Marie-Ève Tremblay**

Owlkids Books

Wisecracker,
firecracker,
knucklecracking
crook.

Codecracking
jackpotter—

look at all he took!

Wiseacre,
worldshaker,
safecracker
Jack.

Found himself
a safe
no other nut
could
crack.

Lipsmacker used a cracker, caught himself **a duck.**

Taught it to use firecrackers, bless his **luck.**

Put it in
the bank vault
deep inside
a sack.

Firecrackers,
ducky going,

**quack
quack
quack**.

Waited till the bank had closed,
troublemaking Jack.

Snuck inside
the vault room
and listened
for the...

crack!

Duck, he blew the door off,
hit the knucklehead **a-smack**.

60

Heartbroken
safecracker,
sore, sad sack.

50

Whoever thought a duck
could crack poor Jack?

40

30

CRACKERJACK
JACK
618-53507-34

Duck, he's full of soda crackers. Eats them all the time.

Dreams of using
firecrackers

for his next big crime.

Owlkids Books acknowledges the financial support of the Canada Council for the Arts, the Ontario Arts Council, the Government of Canada through the Canada Book Fund (CBF) and the Government of Ontario through the Ontario Media Development Corporation's Book Initiative for our publishing activities.

Published in Canada by
Owlkids Books Inc.
10 Lower Spadina Avenue
Toronto, ON M5V 2Z2

Published in the United States by
Owlkids Books Inc.
1700 Fourth Street
Berkeley, CA 94710

Library and Archives Canada Cataloguing in Publication

Wilker, Bowman, author
    Crackerjack Jack / written by Bowman Wilker ; illustrated by Marie-Ève Tremblay.

ISBN 978-1-77147-244-9 (hardcover)

    I. Tremblay, Marie-Ève, 1978 July 19-, illustrator II. Title.

PS8645.I4354C73 2018   jC813'.6   C2017-903875-3

Library of Congress Control Number: 2017943553

Edited by: Karen Li and Sarah Howden
Designed by: Danielle Arbour

Manufactured in Shenzhen, China, in September 2017, by C&C Joint Printing Co.
Job #HR4254

A   B   C   D   E   F

Publisher of Chirp, chickaDEE and OWL
www.owlkidsbooks.com | Owlkids Books is a division of Bayard CANADA